Mrs. Redcat
3 Mousehole Lane
Whiskerville

Orchard Books, A Grolier Company, 95 Madison Avenue, New York, NY 10016

Manufactured in the United States of America
The text of this book is set in 18 point Cochin. The illustrations are watercolor.
Printed and bound by Phoenix Color Corp.   10 9 8 7 6 5 4 3 2 1

Library of Congress Cataloging-in-Publication Data
Aggs, Patrice.
The visitor / by Patrice Aggs.   p.   cm.
Summary: Two young cats, whose dinner guest is a giraffe, are not sure they want to meet this unusual stranger, but they change their minds after getting to know him.
ISBN 0-531-30059-5 (trade : alk. paper).—ISBN 0-531-33059-1 (lib. bdg. : alk. paper)
[1. Cats—Fiction.   2. Giraffe—Fiction.   3. Individuality—Fiction.]   I. Title.
PZ7.A2675Vi   1999   [E]—dc21   97-8195

The VISITOR

by PATRICE AGGS

Orchard Books • New York

"**W**e are going to have a visitor!" said Mrs. Redcat one morning.

"Is it Grandma?" asked Cosy.

"Is it Cousin Pie from Mousehole?" asked Posy.

"It's Giraffe," answered their mother.

"Will he sleep here?" asked Cosy.

"Will we have to get dressed up?" asked Posy.

Mrs. Redcat laughed. "He's coming for dinner. Today," she said.

Cosy and Posy told Mrs. Tabby Next Door.
"What's a giraffe like?" they asked her.
"I've never met a giraffe," she replied.
"All I know is that it's an animal."
"Like Mouse?" asked Cosy.

But when they asked Mouse, he said, "A giraffe isn't like me at all. A giraffe has a very long neck, like Goose."

But when they told Goose that a giraffe was coming to visit, with a long neck like hers, she said, "He may have a long neck, but he's not like me. A giraffe has spots, like Ladybird."

But when they told Ladybird that a giraffe was coming to visit, Ladybird said, "He might have spots, but he's not like me. A giraffe eats leaves on trees, like Caterpillar."

But when they told Caterpillar that a giraffe was coming to visit, Caterpillar said, "He might eat leaves, but he's not like me at all. A giraffe is very, very tall."

"Tall?" Cosy wondered. "As tall as a beech tree?"

"Oh no," said Caterpillar. "But a giraffe is taller than *any* animal you've ever seen."

"Does he have a very long neck?" asked Cosy.

"He's got a longer neck than *any* animal you've ever seen," Caterpillar said.

"And spots?" Posy whispered. "Does he have more spots than Ladybird?"

"A giraffe," Caterpillar said solemnly, "has more spots than *any* animal you've ever seen."

"Cosy! Posy!" called Mrs. Redcat. "Time to come in."

Cosy and Posy started home, but not very quickly.

"Come on," said Mrs. Redcat. "I want your paws washed before our visitor arrives."

"I don't like visitors," Cosy told her.

"Not visitors with spots," Posy remembered.

"Or long, scary necks," Cosy whispered. "I don't think we're coming in."

Mrs. Redcat put a look on her face.

Cosy and Posy went in.

And then Giraffe arrived.

They had dinner.

After dinner . . .

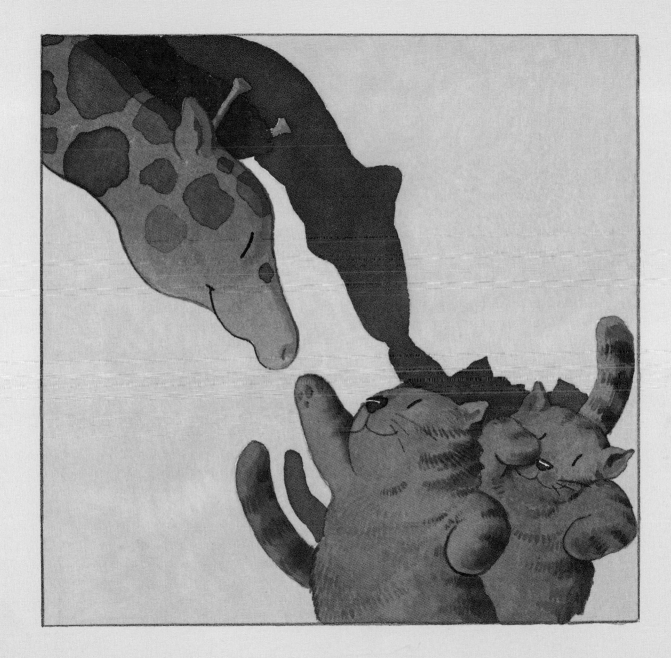

Giraffe's long neck turned out to be fun.

"I don't think I mind long necks," said Cosy.
"Or spots—"

"I don't think I mind visitors!" Posy
interrupted.

In fact, the only thing they
both minded was . . .

it was only a visit, and it was time for their visitor
to say good-bye!